What Should DANNY DO?

Ganit & Adir Levy

Illustrated by Mat Sadler

Hi! My name is Danny.

My favorite things in the whole world are soccer, superheroes, and ninjas. I also love skateboards, but I don't have one yet.

You may be wondering why I'm wearing a cape, so I'll let you in on my secret: I'm a superhero in training. That means I have *some* superpowers, but I'm still working on the rest.

For example,
I jump super high.

I run super fast.

I have super muscles.

And even though I can't fly just yet...

I'm still working on it.

Daddy says that my most
important superpower of all
is my POWER TO CHOOSE. With
this power, I can change my day by
changing my choices. He even gives me
the coolest cape so that I won't forget.

Today is a special day because you'll be making choices for me! When you get to the end of the day, you can start over and make different choices. Then we'll see if the POWER TO CHOOSE really does change my day.

Ready? Lets go!

Mmmm! Do I smell pancakes?
I *love* pancakes.

I zoom downstairs.

"*Chocolate chip pancakes!!!*" I yell.

But then I see my brother Charlie eating from our Ninjitsu Ninja plate. That plate is my favorite.

"I want the ninja plate!" I say.

"I know you love that plate," Mommy says, "but Charlie is already eating from it." She puts two pancakes in front of me, but they're on an alphabet plate. I already know my alphabet.

What Should DANNY Do?

Eat the pancakes on the alphabet plate? Go to page 26
Yell until he gets the ninja plate? Go to page 16

I run over and push Charlie into the mud. His foot gets tangled in mine, so I fall into the mud too. *Eewww!*

Mommy hears us yelling and comes outside. Charlie tells her that I pushed him down.

"Daniel," Mommy says, "you need to go inside and calm down. And no more backyard playtime for the rest of the day."

Nooooo! That means I won't get to swim, or play in the treehouse, or practice flying!

I go to my room.

I feel like my superpowers have been wiped out. I think about all the bad things that happened today because of the choices I made. Maybe I need to practice using my POWER TO CHOOSE so that my day doesn't end up like this tomorrow.

End #3

I summon my super strength and "Hi-ya!"

BOOM! CRASH!

The track breaks into pieces.

Mommy comes into the living room.

"What happened here?" she asks.

"Danny kicked it down!" Charlie cries.

"I was planning on taking you to the park, but now you'll be staying home to think about how you've behaved," she says. "Please clean this mess up, boys."

Cleaning up toys I didn't even play with is no fun. *And I* don't get to play soccer at the park!

I think about what Mommy said. I know I wouldn't be happy if Charlie knocked down a track I built.

After lunch, Charlie is playing the Ninjitsu Ninja video game.

"I wanna play!" I tell him.

"Wait till I finish this game," he says.

I wait and wait and wait for like a thousand minutes!

"You're taking too long. Let me play," I say as I reach for the controller.

"I'm not done yet!" Charlie yells. He elbows my hand away.

What Should DANNY Do?

Wait until Charlie is done with his game? Go to page 64
Grab the controller out of Charlie's hands? Go to page 66

I yell. I stomp. I scream.

"No faaaaaiiiiiirrr!

I want the ninja plate!" I say.

It isn't helping.

I push the alphabet plate away from me. My super
muscles are so strong that the plate zooms into the
pitcher of orange juice. *Oops!* It spills everywhere!
Orange juice on the table.
Orange juice on the floor.
Orange juice on my pancakes.
Yuck!

Mommy hands me a towel. Great. Now my pancakes are ruined, *and* I have to clean up the mess.

Wiping up the juice takes forever, and now I'm stuck with cereal. Cereal doesn't charge my super muscles like pancakes do.

I finish eating and see Charlie playing with our new race car set. I wanted to race the cars!

Charlie licks his fingers loudly with a smirk on his face. I think he's making fun of me for not getting pancakes!

What Should DANNY Do?

Knock the race car set down? Go to page 12
Find a way to play with Charlie? Go to page 30

33
51
57

We quickly clean up, then go to the park.

I use my super speed to zoom around.

Woosh!

Then I hear my favorite music in the world.
I know exactly where it's coming from!

"Can we please, please, please have some ice cream, Mommy?" I beg.

"Sure," she says.

Score! I choose my favorite, an ice cream sandwich. Charlie chooses a rainbow snowcone. I tell him to eat quickly so that we can go play soccer.

He pushes his cone up to take a bite, but it slips out and falls in the mud! *Ewww!*

Charlie starts to cry.

What Should DANNY Do?

Eat his ice cream quickly before Charlie can ask for some? Go to page 48

Share some of his ice cream with Charlie? Go to page 44

Mommy isn't happy with how I've behaved, so now I'm stuck at home all day!

After lunch, I have to clean my room. Cleaning my room is no fun when I know I could have been at the park instead.

Later, my tummy begins to rumble like a bulldozer. That means I'm hungry. If I ask Mommy for a snack, she'll probably give me something healthy. But I think my superpowers need chocolate to recharge.

Mommy thinks I can't reach the top of the pantry where she keeps the candy. She doesn't know I can climb like a super spider.

What Should DANNY Do?

Ask Mommy for a snack? Go to page 62
Sneak some chocolate from the pantry? Go to page 58

"But, can I get the Ninja plate next time?" I ask.

Mommy smiles and says, "Of course."

The pancakes are dee-licious! I can feel them charging my super powers with every bite.

After we finish, Mommy tells us to get ready because we're going to the park! *Score!* I *love* the park!

"Do you want to set up a lemonade stand while we're there?" Mommy asks.

"Yes!" I say.

"No way!" Charlie pouts. "I want to play at the park, not work!"

Mommy tells Charlie that he can play, but he won't get to share the money if he doesn't help me.

I quickly get dressed, then make a big "LEMONADE" sign.

I get ten lemons,
two pitchers, and
lots of sugar.

I'm lucky I have
the super muscles
to carry it all.

I squeeze the lemons, but the last one is really hard. I summon my super strength and finally get the juice to come out.

But then, oops! The juice squirts right into my eye!

"OWWW!" It stings so much I start to cry. Charlie laughs at me.

What Should DANNY Do?

Stomp really hard on Charlie's foot? Go to page 56
Tell Charlie that isn't nice? Go to page 34

I'm bothered by Charlie's teasing, but I let it go because it's not a big deal. After all, I was the one who ruined my pancakes.

"You're lucky you got pancakes," I say. "Do you want to build a quadruple loop crash track together?"

Charlie thinks, then says, "Yeah!"

Together we build the coolest crash track ever.

"1, 2, 3!!!"

We both let go of our race cars at the same time.

SMASH! CRASH!

The cars crash in mid-air!

We test them all. Blue Lightning Bolt and Red Rocket Racer are the fastest. We crash them a hundred times!

Mommy comes into the living room and tells us to get dressed because we're going to the park. *Score!* I *love* the park.

But when Charlie comes back I see that he has brand new shoes!

"How did you get those?" I ask.

"Mom got them for me because my old ones had a hole," he answers.

No fair, I want new shoes too!

What Should DANNY Do?

Yell at his mom for not buying him new shoes? Go to page 50
Tell Charlie how cool his new shoes are? Go to page 68

"Laughing at me isn't nice," I tell Charlie.

Mommy is happy I used my words to let Charlie know how I feel. She helps me rinse my eye, and the sting slowly goes away.

I finish making the lemonade, and Mommy lets me have a whole glass. Mmmm! That makes my eye feel even better.

We get to the park, and Charlie runs off to play.

At first, no one wants my lemonade. But then a great idea pops into my head! I use my laser beam focus to turn the plain lemonade into Super Lemonade!

super
Lemonade

50¢

I shout as loud as I can, "Fresh squeezed Super Lemonade, only 50 cents! Drink some and get a superpower for the day!"

My idea works! After an hour, I have just one cup left.

I see a girl running towards me. I use my mind reading ability to see that she wants a superpower of her own.

But then, *oops!* She trips and knocks my table down. The last cup of lemonade spills all over my shirt.

What Should DANNY Do?

Help the girl up? Go to page 38
Yell at the girl for spilling his last cup? Go to page 42

I help the girl up.

"I'm so sorry," she says.

"Don't worry," I tell her. "It was just an accident."

Her mom pays me a whole dollar for the cup she spilled, even though my mommy says she doesn't have to.

Score! I made $26.00 from the lemonade stand. I remember to set $3.00 aside for charity, so I have $23.00 left.

Mommy surprises me and takes me to the toy store because of how good I've been today.

I know exactly what I want to get, and I've made just enough money to buy it!

SKATEBOA

I get home and ride my skateboard down the street.
Wow, I'm finally flying!

My best friend Jakey sees me and says, "Whoa, Danny!
How did you get that cool skateboard?"

I tell him about my superpower lemonade and offer to help him
make some next week. He's super excited.

"I'm proud of how you've used your POWER TO CHOOSE today, Danny," Mommy says. "So, I'll let you make one more choice: what we'll have for dinner."

Hmmm. I wonder what food will charge...

End #1

"You spilled my last cup!" I yell.

"I'm sorry," she says. "It was just an accident."

"I don't care. You have to pay me for it!"

She looks at me and starts to cry. Mommy helps the girl up and says, "You don't need to pay for that cup, sweetie."

"But she knocked it over!" I yell.
"It's her fault I can't sell it!"

Mommy isn't happy with me.

"I was going to take you to the toy store so you could pick something out with the money you made," she says. "Instead, we'll be going home."

I pack up the stuff from the lemonade stand and get into the car.

"Our day went really well until just now, Danny. How would you have felt if you were that girl?" Mommy asks.

I think about how I made her feel. Mommy is right. I wish I could take back my last choice and treat her nicely. I think my day would have ended much better.

End
#4

Charlie looks so sad. I take one last bite of my ice cream sandwich and hand him the rest. He stops crying and smiles.

Mommy says, "I saw what you just did, Danny, and I'm so proud of you." She gives me a big hug and that makes me feel good.

As soon as Charlie finishes, we run to play soccer.

"I'll be goalie first because you gave me some of your ice cream," Charlie says.

After a while, the game is tied 9-9. I know I need my superpowers to score the last goal. I run back as far as I can...

Hi-ya!

I unleash a super kick. The ball goes so fast it almost tears through the net! *Yes!* I win!

Mommy tells us she's proud of how nicely we shared at the park.

On the ride home, we have a great time playing Superheroes vs. Ninjas together.

After dinner and a bath,
Mommy comes to tuck me in.

"Isn't it nice to see how the day got better
as you made better choices?" she asks.

"Yes, Mommy."

She smiles and gives me a kiss. "Good
night, Danny. I love you."

"Good night, Mommy. I love you too."

End
#5

I eat my ice cream sandwich so fast that I get a brain freeze. Aw, man, I hate brain freezes! Last time I had one my super powers froze for a whole hour!

Mommy saw what happened, so she buys Charlie a new snow cone.

When he finally finishes, we argue because neither of us want to be goalie first. We end up playing by ourselves, and that isn't very fun. Scoring goals without a goalie is too easy for a superhero like me.

On the ride home, Charlie and I are still upset and hardly say a word to each other.

At dinner, Daddy asks me if I had a good day.

"Not really," I say.

"Do you think you used your POWER TO CHOOSE wisely?" he asks.

Hmmm. Maybe if I practice my POWER TO CHOOSE as much as I practice flying, my days really will be better.

End #6

I stomp over to mom. "That's not fair! How come Charlie got new shoes and I didn't? I want new shoes too!"

"I understand that you really want new shoes, Danny," Mommy says. "But Charlie had a hole in his. I will buy you new shoes when you need them."

"But everyone knows superheroes can't wear shoes that smell like stinky fish!" I yell.

"Danny, you need to put your shoes on and clean up with Charlie so that we can go to the park."

Charlie starts cleaning up the race car set, but I'm not sure I feel like helping him.

What Should DANNY Do?

Refuse to clean up until he gets new shoes? Go to page 24
Put on his shoes and clean up? Go to page 20

I come up with a game I think Charlie would like. "Want to play Monkey in the Middle with Oreo?" I ask.

He thinks for a while. "OK," he says. "But I get to throw first." I hand him the frisbee.

After a few throws, Oreo flies super high and catches it! I think my superpowers are rubbing off on my dog. Maybe he should get a cape too.

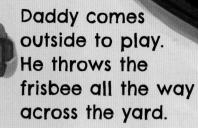

Daddy comes outside to play. He throws the frisbee all the way across the yard.

Charlie and Oreo run to find it.

"How was your day, Danny?" he asks me.

I tell him everything that happened.

"Could you have used your POWER TO CHOOSE to improve your day?"

I think. Maybe I would have gone to the park and done some other fun things if I made better choices.

"Yes, Daddy," I say.

He smiles and gives me a hug. I can tell he is proud that I understand my POWER TO CHOOSE.

End #7

"OOOWWWWW!" Charlie yells. He stomps back on my foot and tries to grab me!

"MEANIE!" I yell.

"RRRRRRAAA!" Charlie roars.

I push him off of me, but my super muscles are too strong. He bumps into the lemonade, and it spills everywhere. Aw, man! Now I can't have a lemonade stand!

Mommy comes in and looks at the mess.

"He started it, *and* he's the one who knocked it over!" I say.

"He pushed me!" Charlie yells.

"Boys," Mommy says, "you need to clean up this lemonade so that we can go to the park."

What Should DANNY Do?

Clean up the lemonade? Go to page 20
Refuse to clean up the lemonade? Go to page 24

I tip-toe to the pantry
and make sure that
no one is looking. Using
my super spider climbing
technique, I get to the top.
I stash a chocolate bar in my
pocket and jump down.

I zoom to my closet and hide. I'm so worried I'll get caught that I eat the chocolate super fast. Chocolate isn't so yummy when you have to gobble it down.

I lick my fingers to get rid of the evidence and go downstairs.

"I see you had some chocolate without my permission," Mommy says.

"No, I didn't," I say.

"Danny, you know you have to ask before having chocolate, and lying to Mommy is not OK."

How does she know?! She must have a super mind reading power of her own.

"Please go to your room and think about how you could've improved the poor choices you made today. And no chocolate cake for dessert tonight."

After a hundred thousand minutes, it feels like I'm trapped in a supervillain's dungeon with no way out! I look outside and see Charlie playing fetch with Oreo. I wish I could play outside!

Daddy comes to my room. "I heard your day wasn't so great, Danny," he tells me. "Every superhero makes mistakes, and that's okay. But the best superheroes learn from their mistakes and use their POWER TO CHOOSE wisely."

I think about how the choices I made led to this bad day. That must be why Daddy says the POWER TO CHOOSE is so important.

End
#8

Mommy makes me ants on a log, but not with real ants. It's yummy and healthy, and it charges my superpowers super fast.

I let Oreo lick my sticky peanut buttery fingers, and like magic, they're all clean!

25

After I'm done, Mommy gets a bath ready just how a superhero likes it: not too hot, not too cold, and filled to the top with bubbles. I jump right in.

"How do you think your day was, Danny?" she asks.

I think about the good things and bad things that happened, and realize that most of it was because of the choices I made. Tomorrow I'll try using my POWER TO CHOOSE to make it a better day.

End
#9

When Charlie is done I get my chance to play. I get a new high score, 143,698! Beat that, Charlie! We take turns playing until our screen time limit is up.

Later, I grab my frisbee and find a new way to zoom downstairs!

I want to play fetch with Oreo, but when I get outside, Charlie is already playing with him.

"Hey, I was going to play with Oreo!" I say.

"Well, too bad." Charlie sneers. "I got here first, so you can't play with him."

What Should DANNY Do?

Push Charlie down? Go to page 10
Find a way they can play with Oreo together? Go to page 52

I swipe the controller out of his hands. Charlie rushes to get it, but before he does, his game is over.

"You lose. My turn," I say.

"No way! You made me lose!" he yells. He jumps at me and tries to wrestle me to the ground. I push him back, but he kicks me in my shin.

"oOOWWW!" I yell.

Just before I unleash my super kick, Mommy walks in.

"What's going on here?" she asks.

"Danny swiped the controller out of my hands!" Charlie yells.

"But Charlie wouldn't let me play!" I say.

"Both of you need to go to your rooms and calm down," Mommy says. "And because you couldn't play nicely, you won't be playing video games tomorrow."

I don't feel like a superhero anymore.

This was the absolute worst day ever! I wonder what I could have done to make it better.

End #2

I'm a little jealous, but I understand that Charlie needed new shoes more than I did.

"Your new shoes are awesome!" I tell him.

"That was really sweet of you, Danny," Mommy says. She reminds us to clean up the race car set so that we can go to the park.

Go to page 20

33

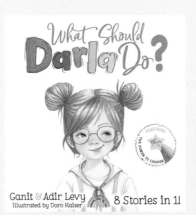

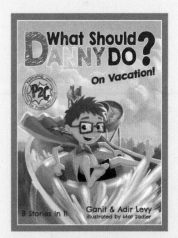

Danny's Second Adventure

Check out our new book, *What Should Danny Do? School Day*, in which Danny learns about his POWER TO CHOOSE! with his friends at school!

What Should Darla Do?

Meet Danny's cousin, Darla! She's a young and spunky astronaut in training, learning all about her POWER TO CHOOSE!

Danny's Upcoming Adventure

What Should Danny Do? On Vacation is coming soon! Check out: whatshoulddannydo.com for more details!

About the Authors

Ganit, a former teacher, and Adir, an astrophysics junkie, are parents to four amazing kids who love learning about how to use their POWER TO CHOOSE wisely.

About the Illustrator

Mat Sadler is an Illustrator of things. He lives with his wife and two kids in England (but he doesn't sound like Hugh Grant—or Pierce Brosnan for that matter. He's from Essex).

Danny

Meet (the real) Danny, the authors' adorable nephew, who served as inspiration for the main character. He's a real superhero in training who never misbehaves. 😜

Danny

Charlie

Mommy

Danny

Daddy

Oreo

Danny

Mommy

Oreo

Dear Parents & Educators,

Children enjoy the book best, and learn the most, when reading through multiple versions of the story. Because this is your child's first exposure to a story in this format, you may need to encourage them to make different choices "just to see what happens."

Through repetition and discussion, your child will be empowered with the understanding that their choices will shape their days, and ultimately their lives, into what they will be.

Ganit & Adir

Danny

Daddy

What Should Danny Do? / by Ganit & Adir Levy.

Summary: Danny, a superhero in training, learns the importance of making good choices.
Levy, Ganit & Adir, authors
Sadler, Mat, illustrator
Klempner, Rebecca, editor
ISBN 978-0-692-84838-8
Visit www.whatshoulddannydo.com
Printed in China
Reinforced binding
Second Edition, July 2017
10 9 8 7 6 5 4

Oreo

Danny

Dear Reader,

There are nine different stories in this book! When you reach an ending, you can start over and make different choices to see how my day changes. The guide below will help you understand the symbols.

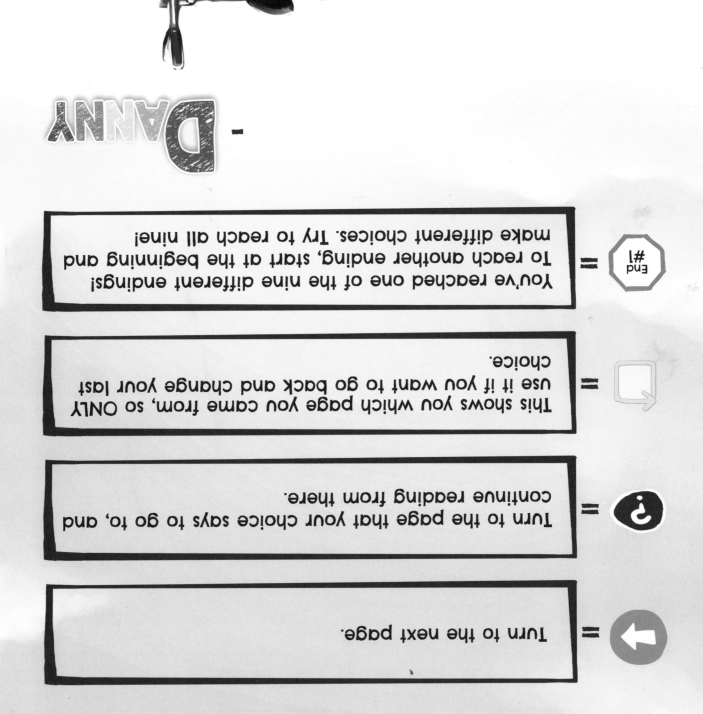

= Turn to the next page.

= Turn to the page that your choice says to go to, and continue reading from there.

= This shows you which page you came from, so ONLY use it if you want to go back and change your last choice.

= You've reached one of the nine different endings! To reach another ending, start at the beginning and make different choices. Try to reach all nine!

- DANNY

Daddy

Danny

Daddy

Danny

Oreo

Danny

Danny

Charlie

Oreo

Mommy

Danny

Oreo

Mommy

Danny

Danny

Charlie

Danny

Daddy

2
12/21

Dear Reader,

There are nine different stories in this book! When you reach an ending, you can start over and make different choices to see how my day changes. The guide below will help you understand the symbols.

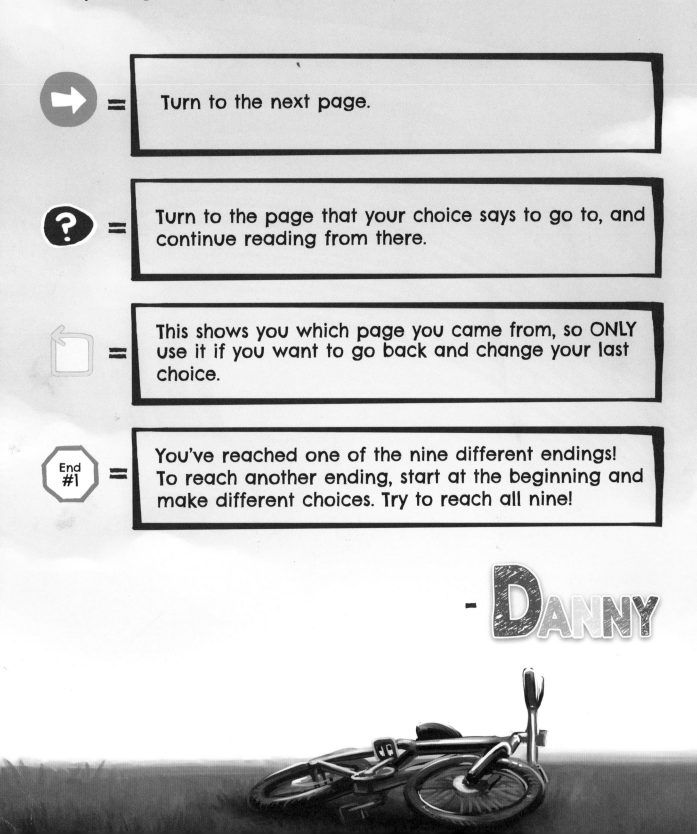

= Turn to the next page.

= Turn to the page that your choice says to go to, and continue reading from there.

= This shows you which page you came from, so ONLY use it if you want to go back and change your last choice.

End #1 = You've reached one of the nine different endings! To reach another ending, start at the beginning and make different choices. Try to reach all nine!

- DANNY

Daddy

Danny

Charlie

Danny

Danny

Mommy

Oreo

Mommy

Oreo

Charlie

Danny

Danny

Oreo

Danny

Danny

Daddy

Danny

Daddy